PLAY TIME!

The THREE BILLY GOATS GRUFF
AND OTHER PLAYS

Books by Julia Donaldson from
Macmillan Children's Books

The Gruffalo
Room on the Broom
The Snail and the Whale
What the Ladybird Heard
The Paper Dolls
The Detective Dog
The Cook and the King
The Woolly Bear Caterpillar
Colours, Colours Everywhere
The Bower Bird
The Tooth Fairy and the Crocodile
Gozzle
Princess Mirror-Belle (a chapter book)
Crazy Mayonnaisy Mum (poetry)
A Treasury of Songs

PLAY TIME!

The THREE BILLY GOATS GRUFF
AND OTHER PLAYS

FOR KEY STAGE ONE

Julia Donaldson

Illustrated by Kate Pankhurst

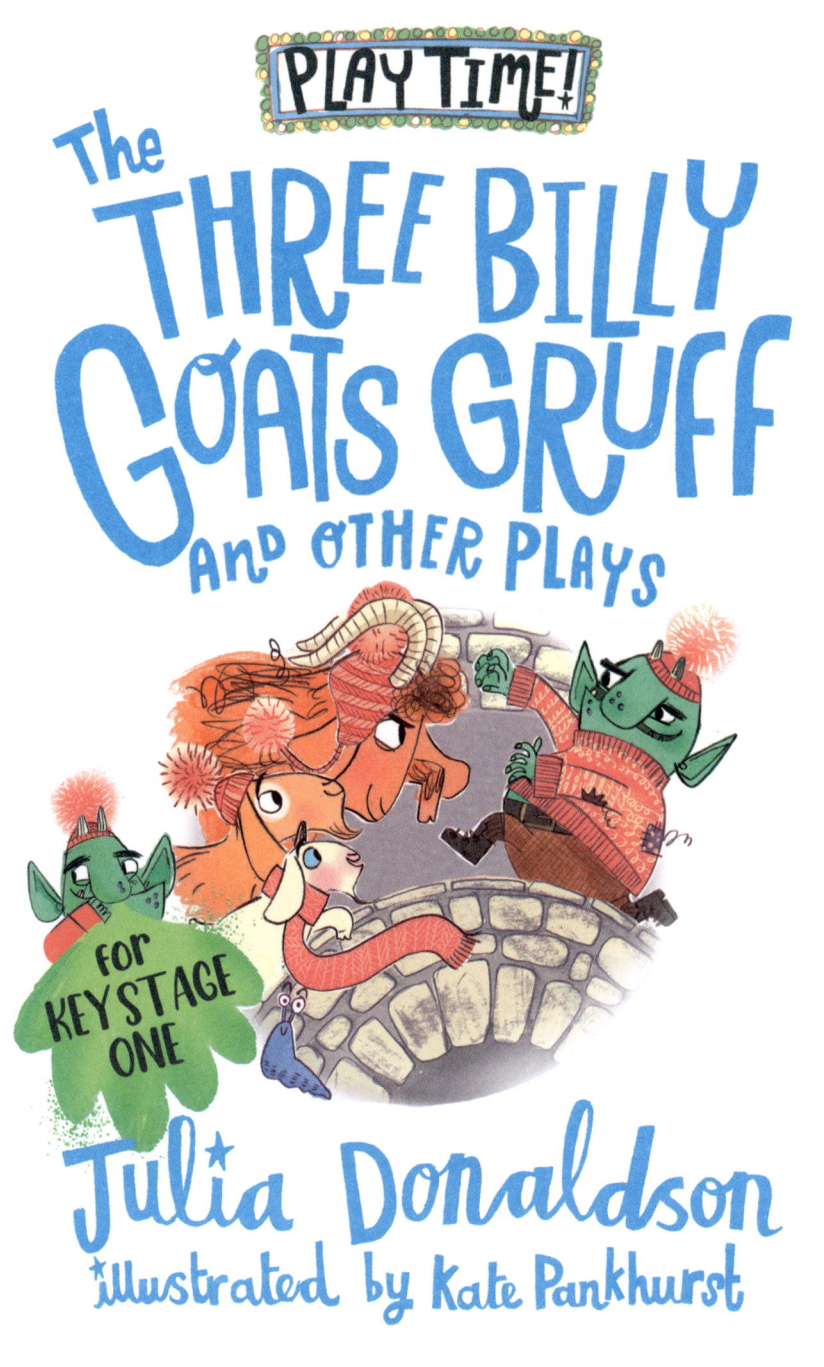

MACMILLAN CHILDREN'S BOOKS

First published 2013 by Macmillan Children's Books as *Play Time*

This edition published 2025 by Macmillan Children's Books
an imprint of Pan Macmillan
The Smithson, 6 Briset Street, London EC1M 5NR
EU representative: Macmillan Publishers Ireland Ltd, 1st Floor,
The Liffey Trust Centre, 117–126 Sheriff Street Upper
Dublin 1, D01 YC43
Associated companies throughout the world
www.panmacmillan.com

ISBN 978-1-0350-1167-4

Text copyright © Julia Donaldson 2013, 2025
Illustrations copyright © Kate Pankhurst 2025

The right of Julia Donaldson and Kate Pankhurst to be identified as the
author and illustrator of this work has been asserted by them
in accordance with the Copyright, Designs and Patents Act 1988.

All rights reserved. No part of this publication may be reproduced,
stored in a retrieval system, or transmitted, in any form or by any means
(electronic, mechanical, photocopying, recording or otherwise),
without the prior written permission of the publisher.

Pan Macmillan does not have any control over, or any responsibility for,
any author or third-party websites referred to in or on this book.

1 3 5 7 9 8 6 4 2

A CIP catalogue record for this book is available from the British Library.

Printed in China

This book is sold subject to the condition that it shall not, by way of trade or otherwise,
be lent, resold, hired out, or otherwise circulated without the publisher's prior consent in
any form of binding or cover other than that in which it is published and without a similar
condition including this condition being imposed on the subsequent purchaser.

Contents

	Author's Note	vi
1.	The Three Billy Goats Gruff	1
2.	The Boy Who Cried Wolf	15
3.	The Magic Twig	31
4.	Turtle Tug	49
5.	Names and Games	69
6.	Birthday Surprise	103
	Putting on a Play	132
	Activities	134
	About the Author and Illustrator	136

Author's Note

This is the first of three collections of short plays for children, designed to be acted or read aloud at school or at home. Most children enjoy acting, and taking part in a play or a play-reading is a fun way of helping them to read more fluently and with expression. Their silent reading improves too, as they learn to keep up and come in at the right time with their lines.

The first four plays, *The Three Billy Goats Gruff*, *The Boy Who Cried Wolf*, *The Magic Twig* and *Turtle Tug*, are all based on traditional tales. They are each for a cast of four and are suitable for a group of beginner readers. I suggest reading the play a few times, at first casting the more able readers in the larger roles but then swapping the parts around. If you like, you can go on to perform the play with simple props or just as a rehearsed reading to the rest of the class. Children love watching their friends acting, and the performing experience really builds up the readers' confidence.

Names and Games, a more contemporary play with a playground setting, is also for four characters and is a little longer and more demanding, and the final play in the collection, *Birthday Surprise*, featuring a spoiled child and a conjuror, is for a group of ten but can be adapted for a whole primary class.

Sometimes children have difficulty knowing when it's their turn to speak, so to make things easier there are symbols, such as a pair of spectacles or a hat, to go with each character's name.

At the end of the book there are some tips and suggestions for activities, in case you are inspired to perform one or more of the plays to a larger audience.

Break a leg!

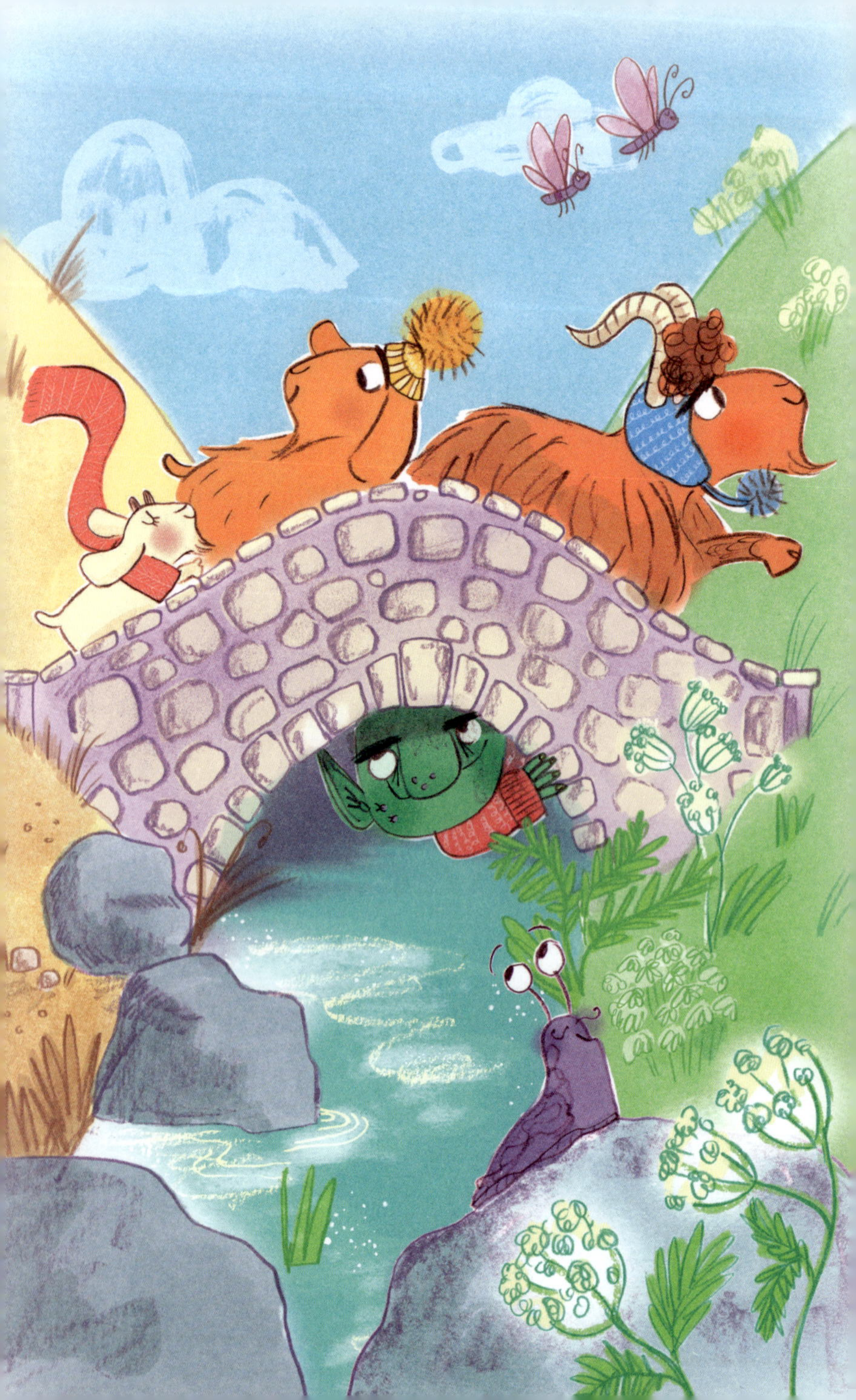

The Three Billy Goats Gruff

Four parts

Suitable for early primary

Characters

Little Billy
Goat Gruff

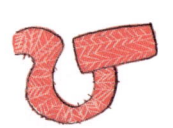

Middle-sized
Billy Goat Gruff

Look out for the symbols to show you who's speaking!

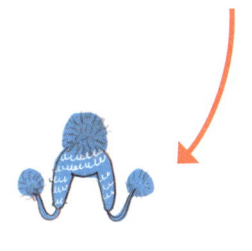

Big Billy Goat Gruff

Troll

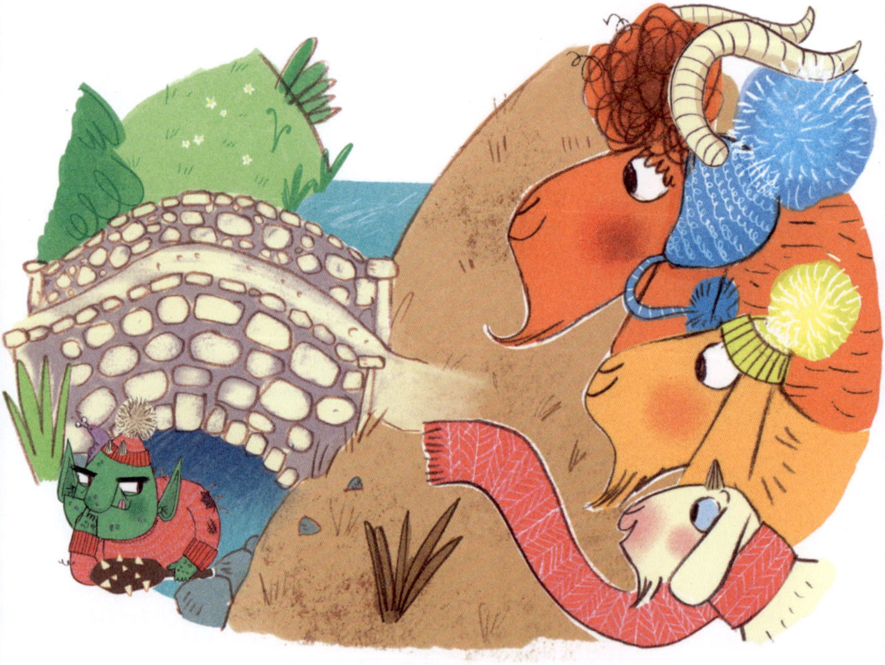

SCENE 1

[The three Billy Goats Gruff are in a field by a bridge. The Troll is lurking under the bridge.]

Little: Hello! I'm Little Billy Goat Gruff.

Middle: I'm Middle-sized Billy Goat Gruff.

Big: I'm Big Billy Goat Gruff.

Troll: I'm a troll.

Little: I like eating grass.

Middle: I like eating grass too.

Big: So do I.

Troll: I like eating goats!

Little: Big Billy Goat Gruff?

Big: Yes?

Little: I don't like this grass.

Big: Why not?

Little: It's all brown.

Big: You're right. It's not very nice.

Middle: But look at that grass over there – that isn't brown.

Little: No, it's green! Let's go and eat it.

Big: Wait!

Middle: Why?

Big: To get to that grass we need to go over the bridge.

Little: So what?

Big: There's a troll under the bridge.

Middle: A troll?

Big: Yes, and he likes eating goats.

Little: Help!

Middle: What can we do?

Big: Just let me think.

Little: I don't like trolls!

Middle: Ssshh! Big Billy Goat Gruff is thinking.

Little: Will he think of something?

Middle: Yes. Now shh!

Big: Come here! This is what we can do!

[They whisper together.]

SCENE 2

[Little Billy Goat Gruff starts to cross the bridge. The Troll pops up.]

Little: *[on the bridge]*
Trip-trap, trip-trap, trip-trap.

Troll: Who's that trip-trapping over my bridge?

Little: It's me, Little Billy Goat Gruff.

Troll: You look good. I'm going to eat you!

Little: Oh no, don't eat *me*! Wait for Middle-sized Billy Goat Gruff.

Troll: Why?

Little: He's bigger than me.

Troll: All right then. I'll wait for him.

Little: Trip-trap, trip-trap, trip-trap.
Green grass, here I come!

Middle: *[on the bridge]*
Clip-clop, clip-clop, clip-clop.

Troll: Who's that clip-clopping over my bridge?

Middle: It's me, Middle-sized Billy Goat Gruff.

Troll: You look good.
I'm going to eat you!

Middle: Oh no, don't eat *me*! Wait for Big Billy Goat Gruff.

Troll: Why?

Middle: He's bigger than me.

Troll: All right then, I'll wait for him.

Middle: Clip-clop, clip-clop, clip-clop. Hello, Little Billy Goat Gruff!

Little: Hello! Have some of this green grass.

Middle: Mmmmmmmm, it's so good!

Big: *[on the bridge]* Tramp-stamp, tramp-stamp, tramp-stamp.

Troll: Who's that tramp-stamping over my bridge?

Big: It's me, Big Billy Goat Gruff.

Troll: You look good. I'm going to eat you!

Big: That's what you think!

Troll: Why, what do *you* think?

Big: I think that I'm going to butt you!

[Big Billy Goat Gruff butts the Troll.]

Troll: Help! I'm falling into the river. SPLOSH!

Big: Tramp-stamp, tramp-stamp, tramp-stamp.

Little: Hello, Big Billy Goat Gruff! Have some of this green grass – it's so good!

Middle: Good old Big Billy Goat Gruff. I said he'd think of something and he did!

Big: That old Troll won't get us now!

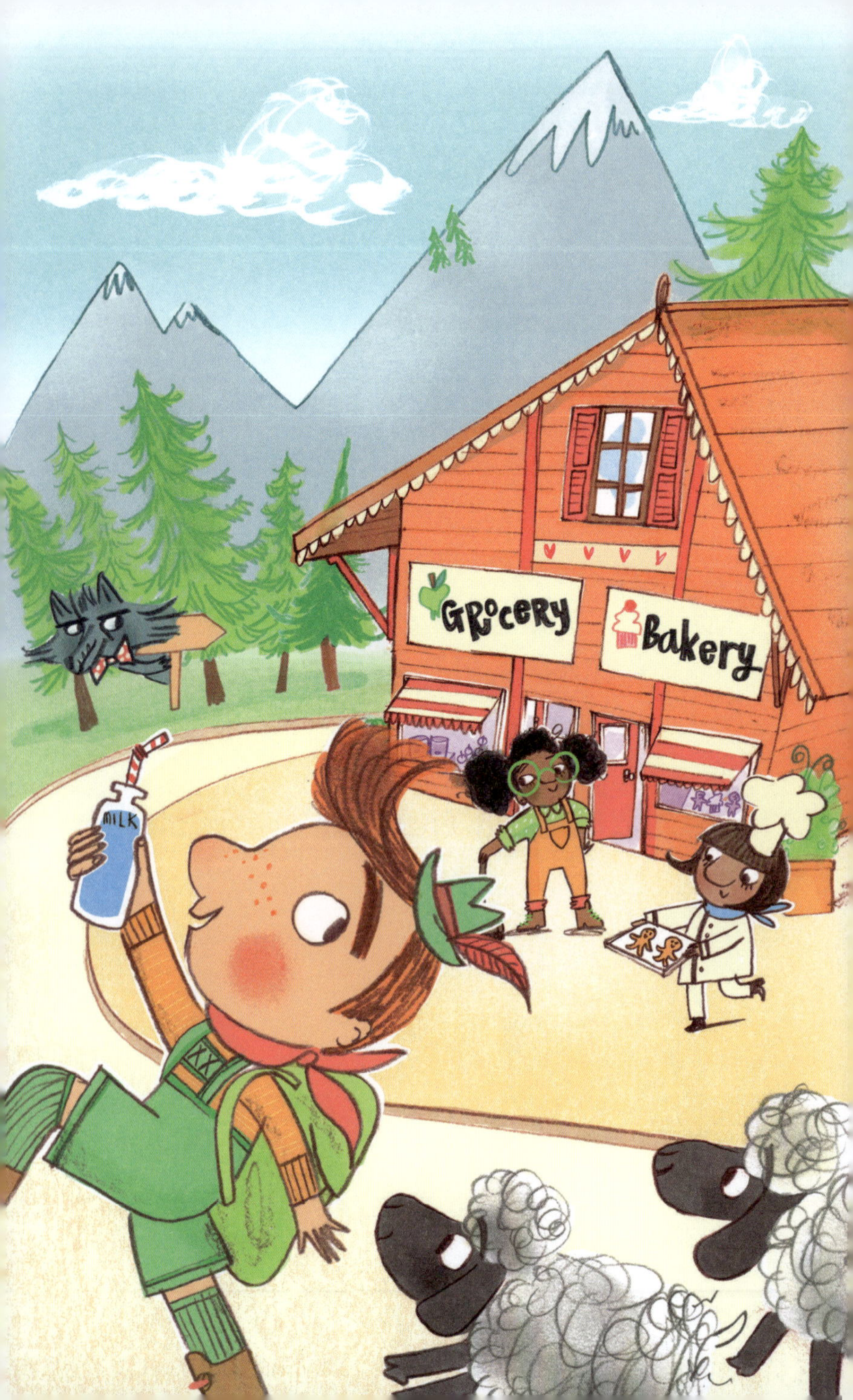
Grocery
Bakery
MILK

The Boy Who Cried Wolf

Four parts

Suitable for early primary

Characters

Shopkeeper

Tom

Look out for the symbols to show you who's speaking!

Wolf

Baker

17

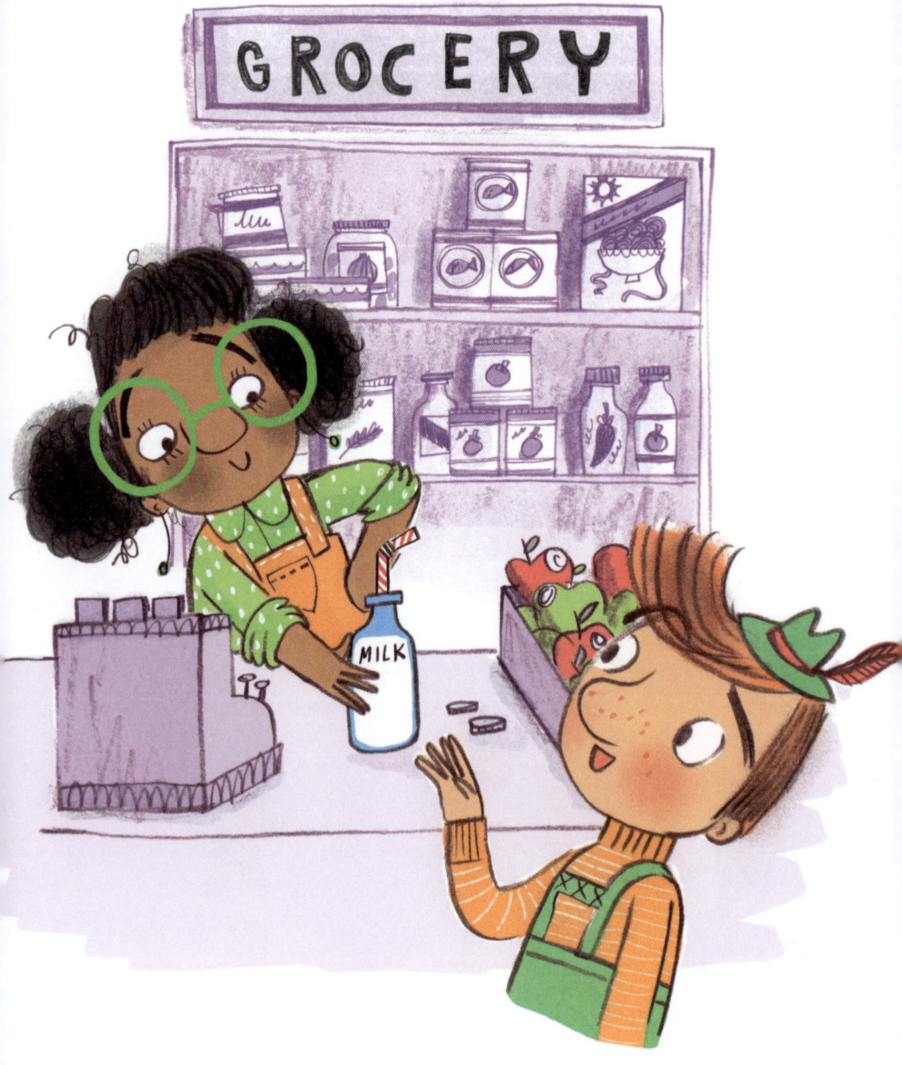
GROCERY
MILK

[There are two shops and a hill nearby. One shop is a bakery and the other a grocer's shop. Tom goes into the grocer's shop.]

Shopkeeper: Hello, Tom. What do you want?

Tom: Some milk for my picnic, please. I'm taking my sheep up the hill.

Shopkeeper: I'd like to be you, up on the hill all day. Here's your milk.

Tom: Thank you. Oh look!

Shopkeeper: What?

Tom: There's a monkey playing with your eggs!

Shopkeeper: Where? I can't see a monkey.

Tom: Ha ha! It was just a trick.

Shopkeeper: You and your tricks! Off you go!

Tom: I like playing tricks!

Wolf: *[hiding]* So do I!

[Tom goes into the bakery.]

Baker: Hello, Tom. What do you want?

Tom: A cake for my picnic, please.

Baker: I wish I could have a picnic too.

Wolf: Me too – a picnic of sheep!

Baker: Here's your cake.

Tom: Thank you. Oh look!

Baker: What?

Tom: There's a giraffe eating your gingerbread!

Baker: Where? I can't see a giraffe.

Tom: Ha ha! It was just a trick.

Baker: You and your tricks! Off you go!

Tom: That was fun! I do like playing tricks.

Wolf: So do I – and I like eating sheep too!

Tom: Come on, sheep! Up the hill!

[Tom goes up the hill with the sheep.]

Tom: Here we are. I'll have my milk, and then I'll play another trick.

[Tom drinks the milk. Then he runs down the hill, shouting.]

Tom: Help! Help! There's a wolf eating my sheep!

Shopkeeper: I'm coming, Tom!

Tom: Quick, quick, run!

Shopkeeper: I am running!

Tom: Here we are!

Shopkeeper: I can't see a wolf.

Tom: Ha ha! It was just a trick.

Shopkeeper: That's not funny.

Tom: Don't be cross. You said you wanted to be up on the hill.

Shopkeeper: I'm going to tell your dad about you.

[The shopkeeper goes away down the hill.]

Tom: That was fun! I'll have my cake now. Then I'll play another trick.

*[Tom eats the cake.
Then he runs down the hill, shouting.]*

Tom: Help! Help! There's a wolf eating my sheep!

Baker: I'm coming, Tom!

Tom: Quick, quick, run!

Baker: I am running!

Tom: Here we are!

Baker: I can't see a wolf.

Tom: Ha ha! It was just a trick. There isn't one.

Wolf: *[hiding]* That's what he thinks!

Baker: That's not funny. I'm going to tell your mum.

Tom: No, don't do that. Go back to your shop. There's a crocodile in there, eating up all the cakes.

[The baker goes down the hill. The wolf comes out of hiding.]

Wolf: Good day to you, Tom.

Tom: Oh no, a wolf. Help!

Wolf: And *I'm* going to have a good day too. I do so like sheep for my picnic.

Tom: No, stop! You can't eat my sheep!

[Tom runs down the hill, shouting.]

Tom: Help! Help! There's a wolf eating my sheep!

Shopkeeper: Oh no there isn't. It's just a trick.

Tom: It's not. I'll go and get my dad.

Shopkeeper: He won't come. I've told him about your tricks.

Tom: Oh no! Help! Help!

Baker: What is it?

Tom: There's a wolf eating my sheep!

Baker: Go away, Tom. You can't trick me.

Tom: I'll go and get my mum.

Baker: She won't come. I've told her about your tricks.

Tom: Oh no! No one will come.

[Tom runs back up the hill.]

Wolf: Hello, Tom. Thank you for the picnic. I do like sheep. Oh look!

Tom: What?

Wolf: There's an elephant eating your hat!

Tom: Where? I can't see an elephant.

Wolf: Ha ha! It was just a trick! Good day to you.

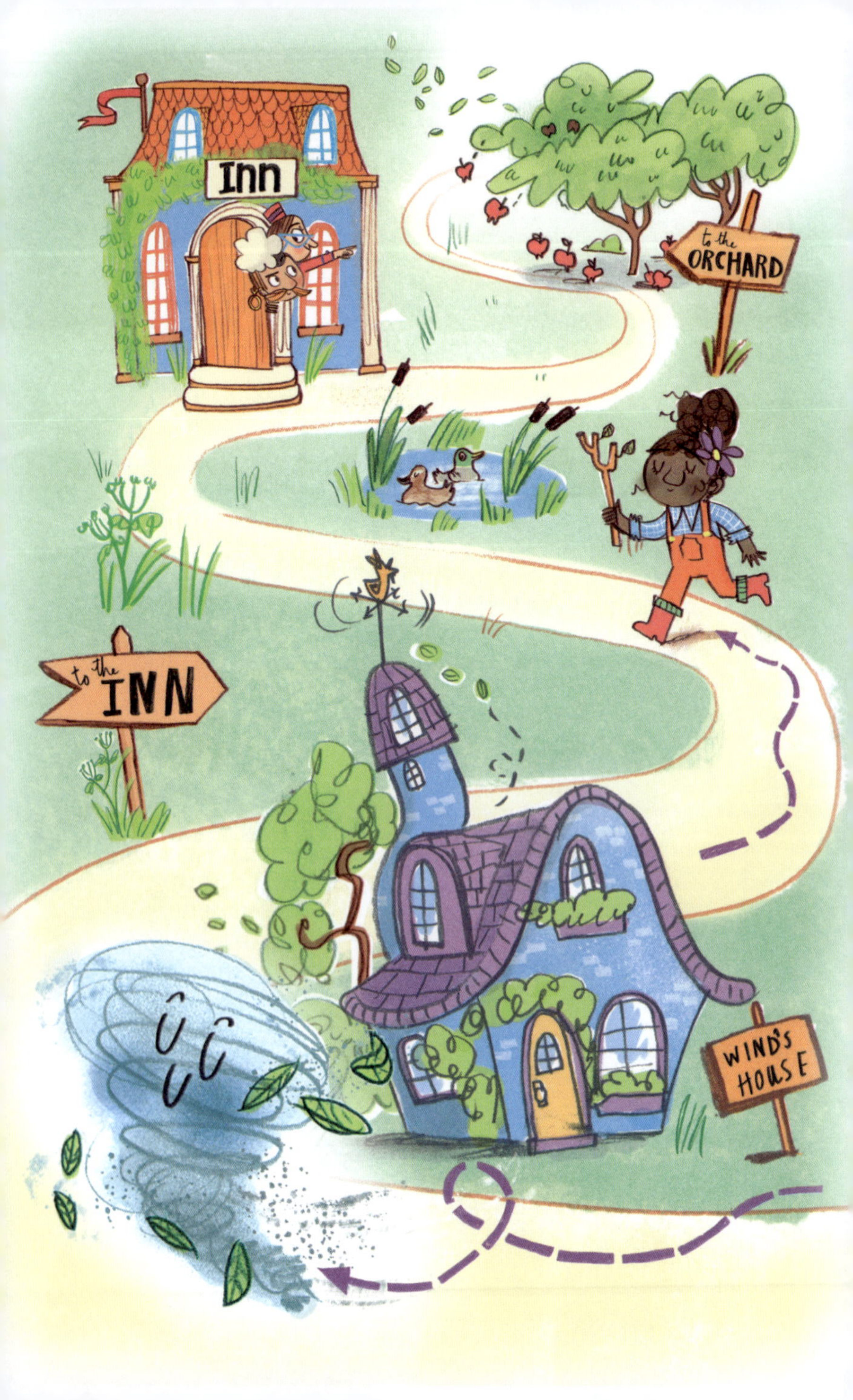
Inn
to the ORCHARD
to the INN
WIND'S HOUSE

The Magic Twig

Four parts

Suitable for early primary

Characters

The Wind

Anna (a farmer)

Look out for the symbols to show you who's speaking!

An Innkeeper

A Cook

33

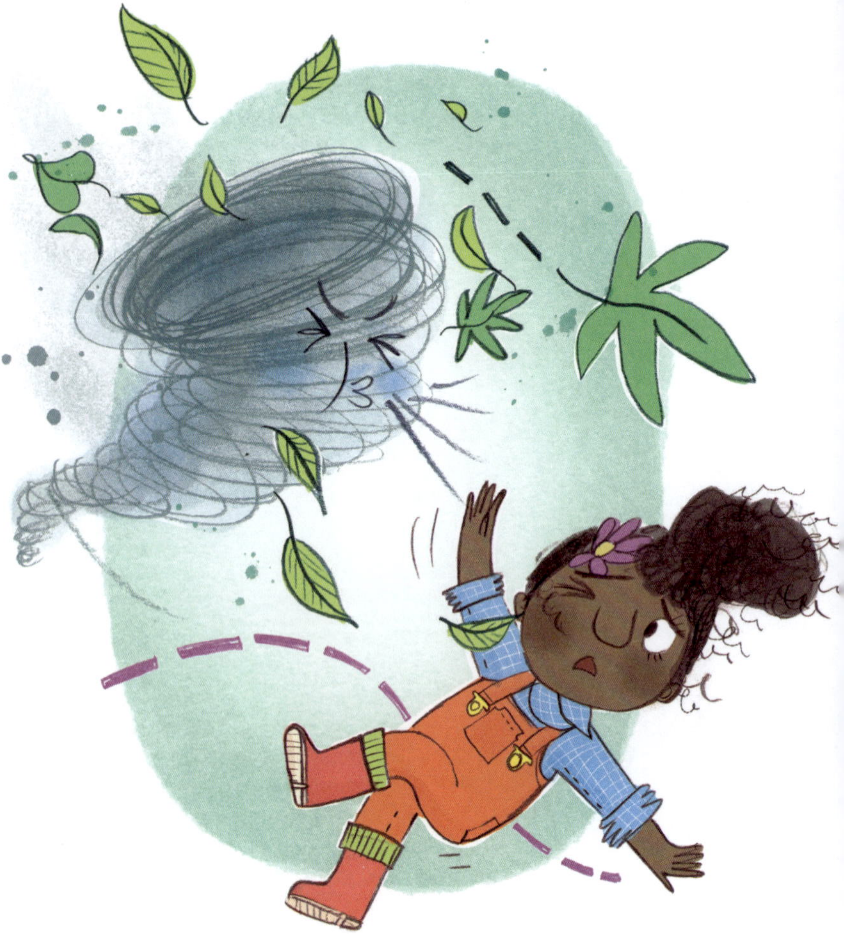

SCENE 1: The Wind's House

[The Wind is running about, blowing. There is a knock at the door.]

Wind: Come in!

Anna: *[coming in]* Hello, Wind . . .

Wind: Blow! Blow! Down you go!
[He blows Anna down.]

Anna: Help! Stop it!

Wind: I'm sorry. I do so like a good blow! Now, what is it?

Anna: It's about my apple trees. All the apples have fallen off. Did you blow them down?

Wind: Me? Apples? Oh yes, I did blow down one or two apples.

Anna: Not just one or two – all of them! They were just little apples. Now I can't sell them.

Wind: Oh dear, I'm sorry. Here, have this.

Anna: A twig? What good is that?

Wind: You'll see. Take it and say:
Little twig, little twig,
Give me apples, red and big.

Anna: Little twig, little twig,
Give me apples, red and big.

Wind: Now look in your pockets.

Anna: Two big red apples! That's magic! Thank you, Wind.

Wind: Go home now, and you'll have apples for ever and ever.

SCENE 2: An Inn

[The innkeeper and cook hear a tap at the door. It is Anna who is on her way home from the Wind's house.]

Innkeeper: Come in!

Anna: *[coming in]* Can I stay here tonight?

Cook: Yes, you can. But what have you got there?

Anna: It's a twig. The Wind gave it to me.

Cook: What for?

Anna: You'll see. Take it and say:
Little twig, little twig,
Give me apples, red and big.

Cook: Little twig, little twig,
Give me apples, red and big.

Anna: Now look in your pockets.

Cook: Apples!

Innkeeper: Big red apples!

Cook: That's magic!

Anna: I'm going to have apples for ever and ever.

Innkeeper: That's good. But you look sleepy now.

Cook: Yes, why don't you go to bed? That's your bedroom.

Anna: Thank you, I will. *[She goes into the bedroom.]*

Innkeeper: Are you thinking what I'm thinking?

Cook: Yes. Let's steal the twig.

Innkeeper: We can swap it for this one.

Cook: Now we'll have apples for ever and ever!

SCENE 3 : The Wind's House

[The Wind is running about, blowing.]

Wind: Blow! Blow! Down you go!
Oh for a good blow!

[There is a knock at the door.]

Wind: Come in!

Anna: *[coming in]* Now look here, Wind...

Wind: Blow! Blow! Down you go!

Anna: Stop that!

Wind: Don't be cross. I did give you the magic twig!

Anna: Yes, but when I got home it didn't work.

Wind: Oh dear. Here, have this.

Anna: A jug of water – what good is that?

Wind: It's magic water. One drop of it can turn into a river. Now you'll have lots of fish for ever and ever.

Anna: Is this a trick?

Wind: No, it's not, And the water can do one other thing.

Anna: What's that?

Wind: It can drown anyone who has played a trick on you.

Anna: I see. Thank you, Wind.

SCENE 4 : The Inn

[There is a knock at the door.]

Innkeeper: Come in.

[Anna comes in.]

Cook: Oh, it's you.

Anna: Hello! What a lot of apples you've got!

Cook: Yes. But what have you got there?

Anna: A jug of water. The Wind gave it to me.

Cook: What for?

Anna: It's magic water. One drop can turn into a river. I'm going to have lots of fish for ever and ever.

Innkeeper: Let's try it in my garden!

Cook: Yes, let's!

Anna: The water can do one other thing.

Innkeeper: What's that?

Anna: It can drown anyone who has played a trick on me.

Cook: Oh help!

Anna: But no one here has played a trick on me, so that's all right. Let's try it now.

Innkeeper: No, please don't!

Anna: Why not?

Innkeeper:	Here, you can have your twig back.	
Anna:	My twig! What, you took it?	
Cook:	Yes, but we're sorry!	
Innkeeper:	Please don't drown us!	
Anna:	All right. But no more tricks!	
Cook:	Thank you, thank you!	
Innkeeper:	Do you want a bed for the night?	
Cook:	Or some food?	
Anna:	No, not in your house! I'm going home to eat lots of fish and apples!	

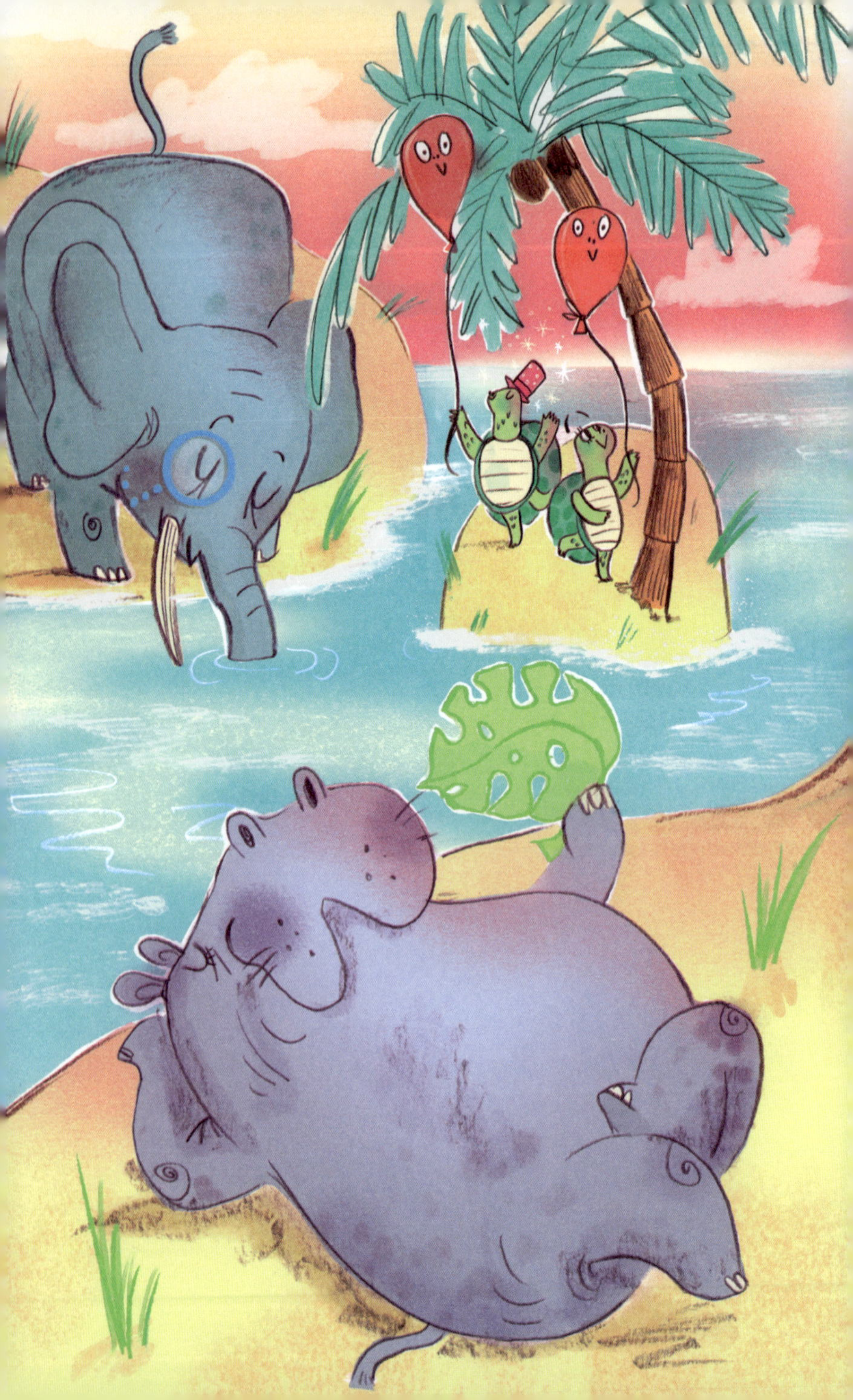

Turtle Tug

Four parts

Suitable for early primary

Characters

Mrs Turtle

Mr Turtle

Look out for the symbols to show you who's speaking!

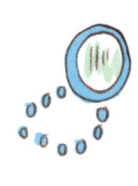

Hippo

Elephant

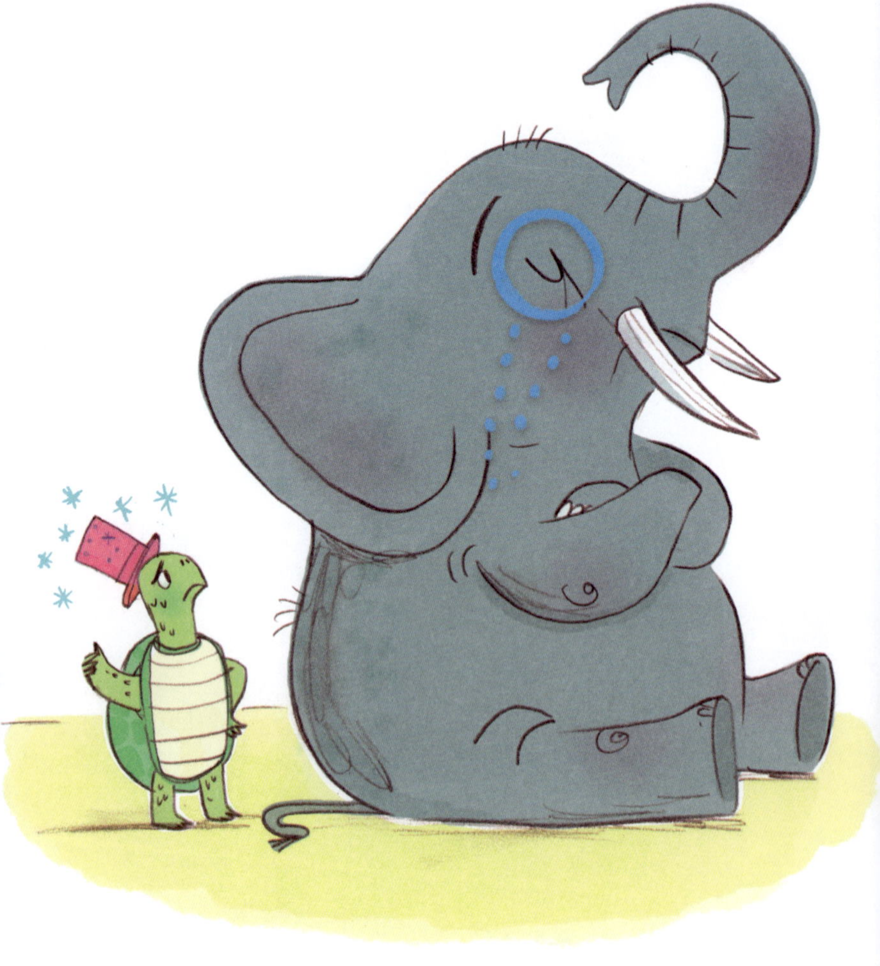

[There is a river with two banks and an island in the middle. Elephant lives on one bank and Hippo on the other. The two turtles live on the island.]

SCENE 1

[Elephant is standing on his riverbank. Mr Turtle swims across to join him.]

Mr Turtle: Hello, Elephant.

Elephant: It's *Sir* Elephant.

Mr Turtle: Sorry, *Sir* Elephant. It's Mrs Turtle's birthday tomorrow. Can you come to her party?

Elephant: Don't be silly, Turtle.

Mr Turtle: I'm not being silly. Mouse can come and Monkey can come. Why can't you?

Elephant: Me? A big strong elephant like me, come to a little turtle's party? No, thank you.

Mr Turtle: All right, Elephant, but you'll miss all the fun.

Elephant: It's *Sir* Elephant, and it's no fun for me to mix with weak little animals like you.

Mr Turtle: If you say so, *Sir* Elephant. Goodbye!

[Mr Turtle swims away.]

SCENE 2

[Hippo is standing on her riverbank. Mrs Turtle swims across to join her.]

Mrs Turtle: Hello, Hippo.

Hippo: Call me *Madam* Hippo.

Mrs Turtle: Sorry, *Madam* Hippo. It's my birthday tomorrow. Can you come to my party?

Hippo: Don't be silly.

Mrs Turtle:		I'm not being silly. Goat can come and Rabbit can come. Why can't you?
Hippo:		Me? A big strong hippo like me, come to a little turtle's party? No, thank you.
Mrs Turtle:		All right, Hippo, but you'll miss all the fun.
Hippo:		It's *Madam* Hippo, and it's no fun for me to mix with weak little animals like you.
Mrs Turtle:		If you say so, *Madam* Hippo. Goodbye!

[Mrs Turtle swims away.]

SCENE 3

[Mr and Mrs Turtle are at home on Turtle Island.]

Mrs Turtle: How did you get on?

Mr Turtle: Mouse can come and Monkey can come, but not Elephant.

Mrs Turtle: Why not?

Mr Turtle: He says he's too big and strong.

Mrs Turtle: He's so snooty!

Mr Turtle: How did *you* get on?

Mrs Turtle: Goat can come and Rabbit can come, but not Hippo.

Mr Turtle: Why not?

Mrs Turtle: She says she's too big and strong.

Mr Turtle: Just like Elephant. How can we stop the two of them being so snooty?

Mrs Turtle: Let me think. Do we have a long rope?

Mr Turtle: Yes.

Mrs Turtle: And a sharp stone?

Mr Turtle: I can find one.

Mrs Turtle: Good. Then I think there is a way!

Turtle Tug

SCENE 4

[Mr Turtle has a long rope. He swims across the river to join Elephant.]

Mr Turtle: Hello, Elephant.

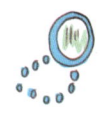

Elephant: It's *Sir* Elephant! What is it now?

Mr Turtle: I'd like to have a tug-of-war with you.

Elephant: Me? A big strong elephant like me, have a tug-of-war with a weak little turtle?

Mr Turtle: I'm just as strong as you!

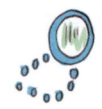

Elephant: Ha ha! All right, we'll try it.

Mr Turtle: Good. Take this end of the rope and when I shout 'Go!' you pull.

[Mr Turtle swims back across the river and meets Mrs Turtle on Turtle Island. He gives her the other end of the rope.]

Mr Turtle: Here's the end of the rope.

Mrs Turtle: Thank you.

[*Mrs Turtle takes the rope and swims to Hippo's bank of the river.*]

Mrs Turtle: Hello, Hippo!

Hippo: It's *Madam* Hippo. What do you want now?

Mrs Turtle: I'd like to have a tug-of-war with you.

Hippo: Me? A big strong hippo like me have a tug-of-war with a weak little turtle?

Mrs Turtle: I may be little but I'm not weak.

Hippo: Ha ha! All right, we'll try it.

Mrs Turtle: Take this end of the rope and when I shout 'Go!' you pull.

[Mrs Turtle swims back to Mr Turtle on Turtle Island.]

Mr Turtle: All right?

Mrs Turtle: Yes.

Mr Turtle: Let's shout then.

Mr and Mrs Turtle: **GO!**

[Elephant and Hippo both pull the rope.]

Elephant: Mr Turtle isn't all that weak.

Hippo: I didn't think Mrs Turtle was so strong!

Turtle Tug

Elephant: I'll have to pull harder.

Hippo: If I don't pull harder, she'll pull me into the river!

Mrs Turtle: Have you got the sharp stone?

Mr Turtle: Here it is.

Mrs Turtle: Good. Let's cut the rope.

[They cut the rope, and Elephant and Hippo both fall over backwards. Mr Turtle swims to Elephant's bank.]

Mr Turtle: Hello, Sir Elephant. Are you all right?

Elephant: Yes thank you, but I got a surprise. You *are* strong, just as strong as me!

Mr Turtle: I said so, didn't I?

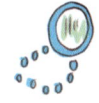

Elephant: Yes, you did. I'm sorry I was so snooty.

Mr Turtle: That's all right, Sir Elephant.

Elephant: You can just call me Elephant.

Mr Turtle: All right then, Elephant. See you at the party!

[Mrs Turtle swims to Hippo's bank.]

Mrs Turtle: Can I help you up, Madam Hippo?

Hippo: Thank you – and you don't have to call me *Madam*. I didn't think you were so strong. I'm sorry I was so snooty.

Mrs Turtle: That's all right, Hippo. So are you going to come to my party?

Hippo: Yes please. And what do you want for your birthday?

Mrs Turtle: How about a new rope!

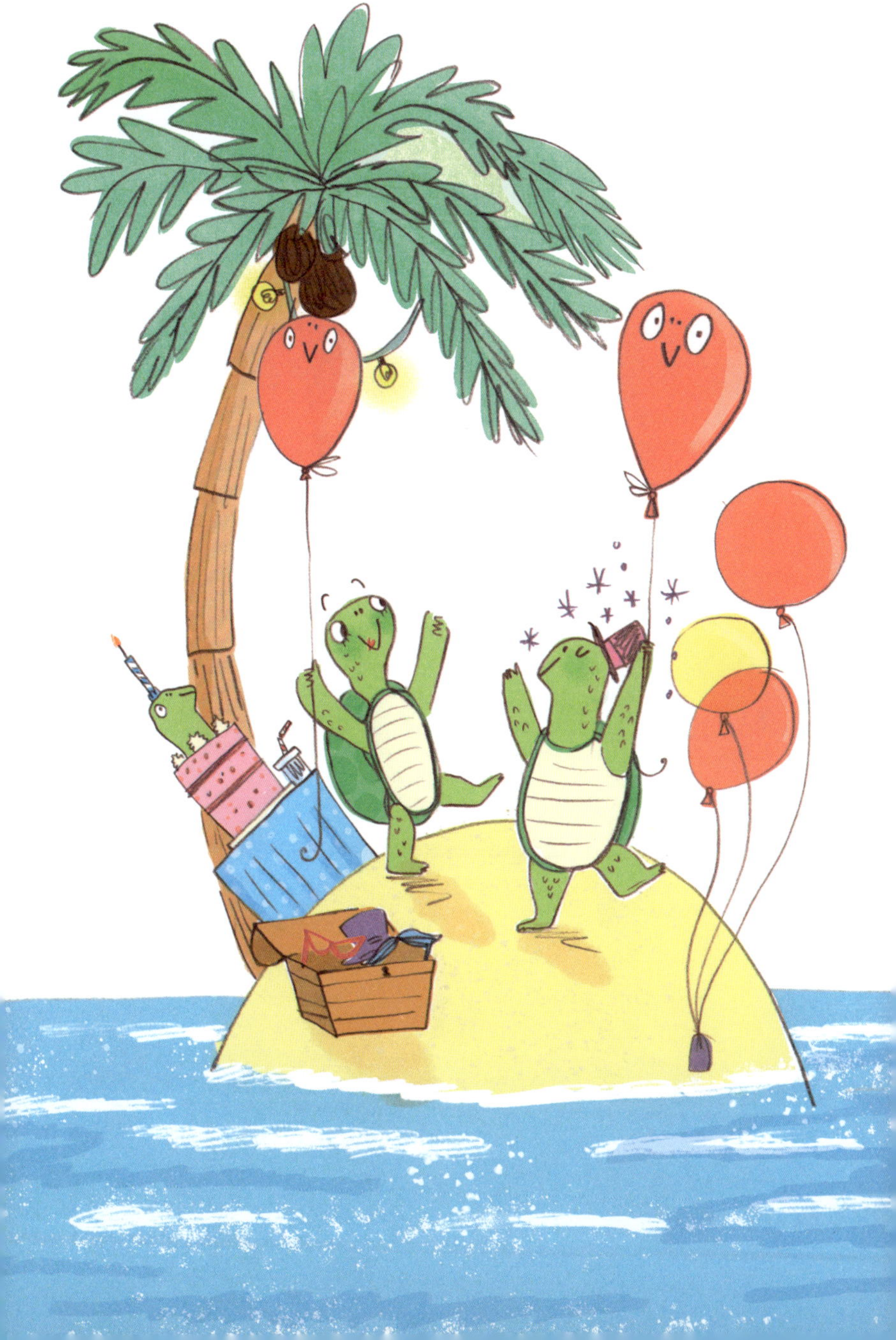

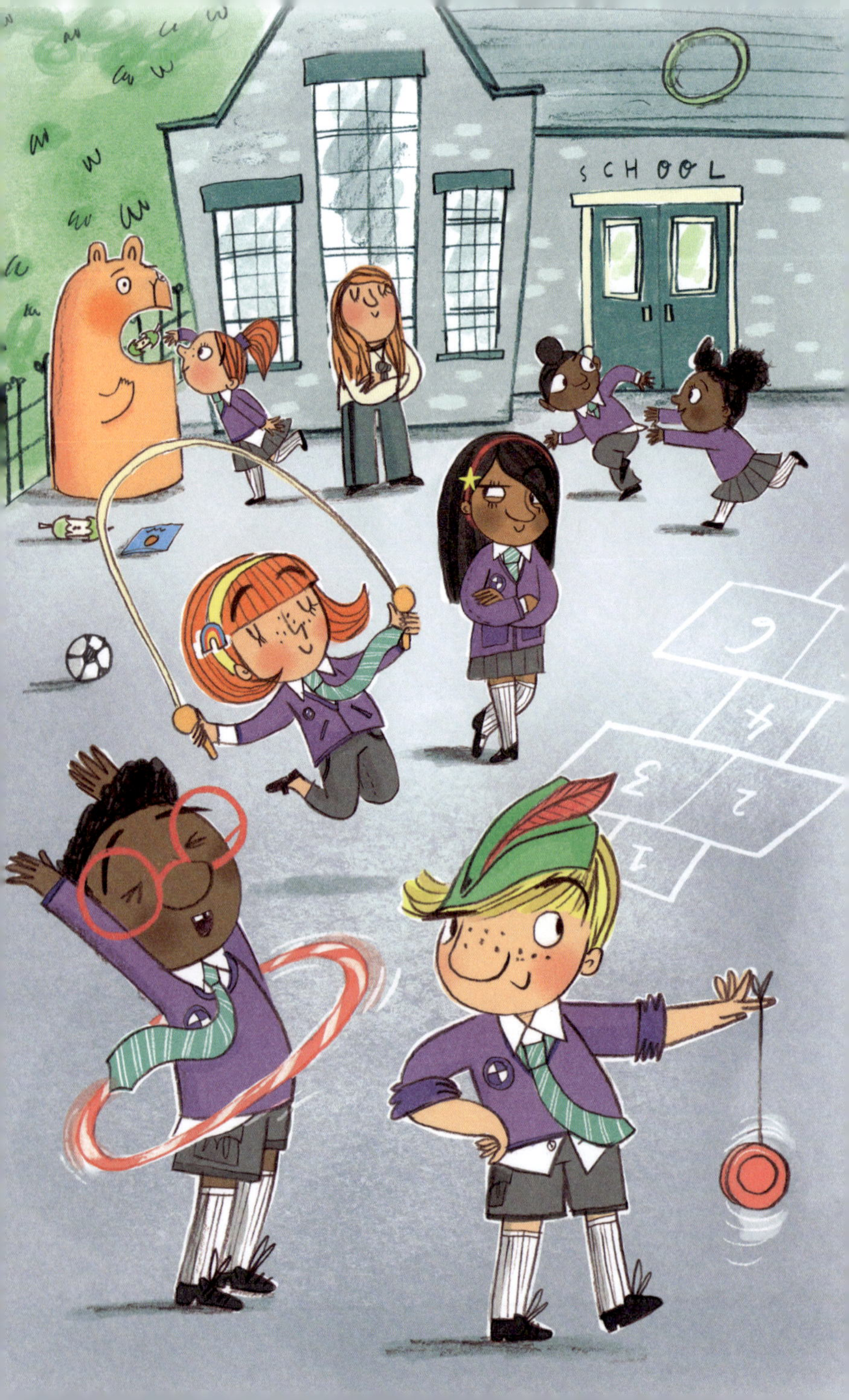
SCHOOL

Names and Games

Four parts

Suitable for middle primary

Characters

Robin
(quite bossy)

Jamie
(Robin's best friend)

Look out for the symbols to show you who's speaking!

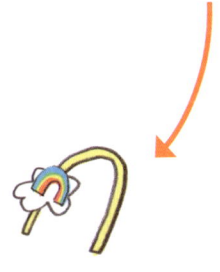

Helen
(sometimes jealous)

Tanim
(Helen's best friend)

Sometimes two characters speak at once so you will see both symbols next to each other like this.

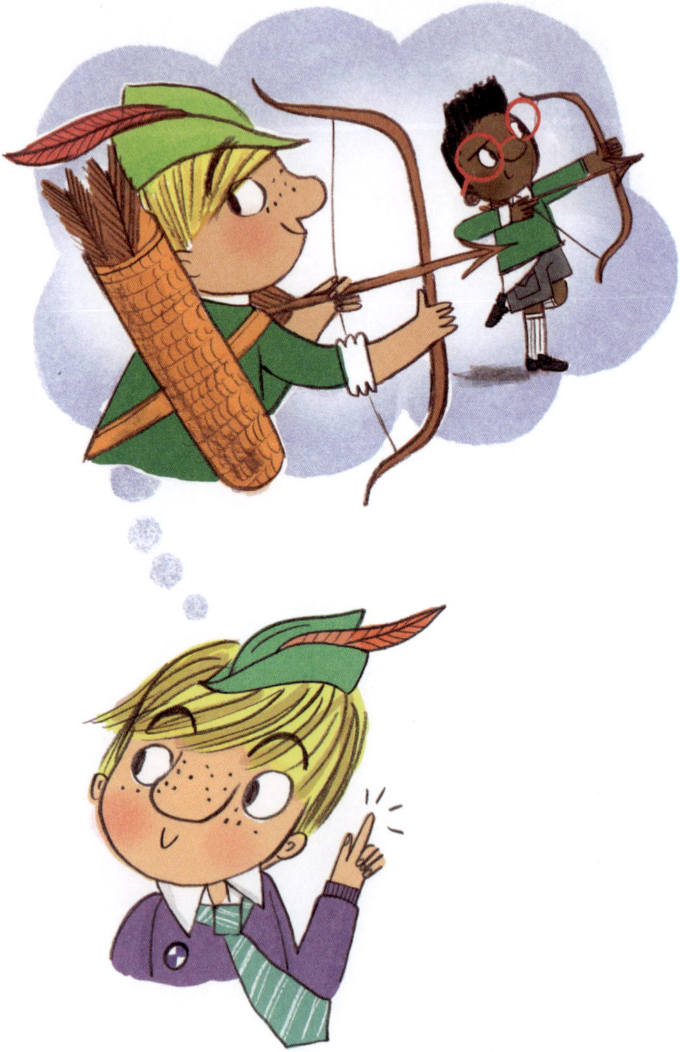

[Each scene of the play takes place in the school playground during a different playtime on the same day.]

SCENE 1: Morning Play
[Enter Robin and Jamie.]

Robin: Hi, Jamie.

Jamie: Hi, Robin. What shall we play today?

Robin: Robin Hood, of course.

Jamie: All right. I'll be Robin Hood then.

Robin: No you can't. I'm Robin Hood. I'm always Robin Hood, remember?

Names and Games

Jamie: That's not fair. Why should you always be Robin Hood?

Robin: Because my name really is Robin.

Jamie: Well, who shall I be then?

Robin: Little John, of course.

Jamie: But I'm sick of being Little John all the time. He just gets bossed about by Robin Hood.

Robin: All right, you can be Friar Tuck then.

Jamie: Who's he?

Robin: He's this fat guy who eats all the time.

Jamie: That sounds more like you.

Robin: I'm not a fat guy.

Jamie: I didn't say you were fat, I just said—

Robin: [noticing Helen and Tanim coming towards them] Be quiet, Little John – someone's coming! Let's hide, then we can spring out on them and take all their gold.

[Robin and Jamie hide. Enter Helen and Tanim.]

Names and Games

Tanim: Hi, Helen.

Helen: Hi, Tanim. What shall we play today?

Tanim: How about Tunnel Tig?

Helen: I've forgotten how you play that.

Tanim: You know, it's that game where you crawl under people's legs to set them free when they've been caught.

Helen: Oh yes, that's good. Who's going to be It?

Tanim: Let's dip. *[She 'dips', starting with Helen.]*
Ibble obble,
Black bobble,
Ibble obble out! I'm It!

Helen: Hey, wait a minute – we can't play that!

Tanim: Why not?

Helen: Well, if you catch me, who's going to crawl under my legs to set me free?

Tanim: We could try and get some more people.

Helen: No, I like playing with just you. Let's think of a different game.

[Jamie and Robin spring out.]

Jamie: Give us all your gold or we'll tie you up!

Robin: No, I say that – I'm Robin Hood, remember?

Jamie: Go on then.

Robin: Give us all your gold or we'll tie you up!

Helen: Go away, you two. We haven't got any gold.

Tanim: We're not playing Robin Hood anyway.

Jamie: What are you playing then?

Tanim: We were going to play Tunnel Tig but we haven't got enough people. Do you two want to play?

Helen: No, we're not having them. Robin's too bossy.

Robin: I don't want to play stupid old Tunnel Tig anyway. Hey, look, Jamie – I mean, Little John – there are some deer over there in the forest! Let's get them!

[Robin and Jamie run off.]

Helen: I know! Let's play bank robbers!

Tanim: How do you play that?

Helen: Well, one person is the bank robber and one person is the banker, and one person is the policewoman . . .

Tanim: But we've only got two people. We can't play that.

Helen: Oh dear.

Tanim: We'll have to get some more people.

[*Jamie and Robin spring out again.*]

Jamie: Run for your lives, you two deer! We're going to shoot you with our bows and arrows!

Robin: No, I have to say that – I'm Robin Hood, remember?

Jamie: Go on then.

Robin: Run for your lives, you two deer! We're going to shoot you with our bows and arrows!

Helen: Go away, you two. We're not deer.

Robin: Yes you are – I just heard you say, 'Oh dear' to Tanim.

Helen: Oh, very funny. Anyway, we've already told you, we're not playing Robin Hood.

Jamie: Why won't you?

Tanim: Yes, let's, Helen. We haven't got enough people for any of our games.

Helen: No, I'm not playing with Robin. I told you, he's too bossy.

Tanim: I like running games.

Helen: All right, race you to the shed, then.

[Helen and Tanim race off.]

Names and Games

Jamie: I managed to shoot those deer, Robin.

Robin: No you didn't, I did. I'm Robin Hood, remember? I'm the best one at shooting arrows. You can cook the deer for our supper if you like.

Jamie: Why don't you cook them?

Robin: I can't cook them, I'm the boss.

Jamie: Well, I've had enough of you bossing me about.

[The bell rings.]

Jamie: There's the bell. And if you think I'm playing Robin Hood again next playtime, you're wrong!

SCENE 2: Lunchtime Play

[Enter Helen and Tanim.]

Tanim: What can we play with only two people?

Helen: Let's play the yes and no game.

Tanim: How do you play that?

Helen: Well, one person asks questions and the other one has to answer them without saying yes or no.

Tanim: All right. I'll ask the questions then. Er . . . is your name Helen?

Helen: It is.

Tanim: And . . . do you like fish and chips?

Helen: I do.

Tanim: Are you my best friend?

Helen: Of course I am.

Tanim: You're too good at this game! Let's think . . . Do you like Jamie?

Helen: He's all right sometimes.

Tanim: Do you like Robin?

Helen: He's much too bossy. Oh no! Here he comes!

[Enter Robin and Jamie.]

Tanim: You just said no! You're out!

Jamie: Hi, Helen. Hi, Tanim.

Tanim: Are you two still playing Robin Hood?

Jamie: No, and I'm not ever playing it again. I'm sick of always being Little John.

Robin: I know, let's play Robinson Crusoe instead. We could all play that.

Helen: No, Tanim's playing with just me.

Tanim: Hold on, Helen. Let's find out how you play it – it could be good.

Robin: Well, Robinson Crusoe gets shipwrecked and he ends up on this desert island. He has a friend called Man Friday. You can be him, Jamie.

Jamie: Why can't I be Robinson Crusoe?

Robin: Is your name Robin or something?

Jamie: What does Man Friday do?

Robin: Well, he sort of follows Robinson Crusoe around and does what he says.

Jamie: This sounds just like Robin Hood.

Robin: It's not a bit like Robin Hood, silly. We're on an *island*. Look, there are sharks all around us! Helen and Tanim can be the sharks.

Names and Games

Helen: No, we're not playing your stupid game.

Tanim: Oh, let's, Helen. It sounds better than the yes and no game.

Helen: All right then.

Jamie: Watch out, sharks, I'm going to harpoon you!

Robin: No, I'm Robinson Crusoe, I have to say that. Watch out sharks, I'm going to harpoon you, and Man Friday will cook you for supper!

Helen: Oh no you won't. We'll eat you for *our* supper!

Robin: No, no, you can't do that!

Names and Games

Tanim: Why not?

Robin: That's not in the story.

Helen: Well, we're changing the story, aren't we, Tanim?

Tanim: Yes, we're going to get you!

[Tanim and Helen start to chase after the boys.]

Robin: No, I'm not playing if you're going to change the story. Come on, Jamie.

Jamie: No, why should I? I'm fed up with you, Robin. It's always, 'Come on, Jamie. Do this, Jamie. Do that, Jamie.' I'm staying here with the girls.

[The bell rings.]

Robin: All right, but I won't play with you next playtime.

Jamie: I don't care. I'd rather play with Helen and Tanim. You're much too bossy, Robin!

SCENE 3: Afternoon Play

[Enter Robin and Jamie.]

Robin: Hi, Jamie. What shall we play?

Jamie: Nothing! I'm playing with Helen and Tanim, remember?

Robin: All right, but don't expect me to play with you ever again. *[He turns away.]*

Jamie: Where are you going?

Robin: Oh, I'll probably go and play football with the big boys.

[He wanders off. Enter Helen and Tanim.]

Tanim: Hi, Jamie. We're going to play 'What's the Time, Mr Wolf?'.

Jamie: Can I be Mr Wolf first?

Helen: Let's see. *[She 'dips', starting with Jamie.]*
Dip, dip.
Sky blue.
Who's It?
Not you!
You're Mr Wolf, Tanim.
Come on, Jamie.

[They walk along behind Tanim.]

Jamie and Helen: What's the time, Mr Wolf?

Tanim: Four o'clock.

Jamie and Helen: What's the time, Mr Wolf?

Tanim: Half past eleven.

Names and Games

Jamie and Helen: What's the time, Mr Wolf?

Tanim: Dinner time! *[She chases them and catches Helen.]* Got you, Helen! Your turn to be Mr Wolf. Come on, Jamie.

Jamie and Tanim: What's the time, Mr Wolf?

Helen: Eight o'clock

Jamie and Tanim: What's the time, Mr Wolf?

Helen: Quarter past five.

Jamie and Tanim: What's the time, Mr Wolf?

Helen: Dinner time! *[She chases them and catches Tanim.]* Got you, Tanim!

[Enter Robin, looking rather miserable.]

Robin: Can I play?

Helen: No! You're too bossy.

Robin: Oh, go on.

Jamie: I thought you were going to play football with the big boys.

Robin: *[rather embarrassed]* They wouldn't let me. They said I was too young, and they said I was . . . oh, never mind.

Tanim: What did they say you were?

Robin: They said I was a rotten runner.

Helen: Well, you are! Robin is a slowcoach, Robin is a slowcoach!

Jamie: Don't be mean. He's not a slowcoach.

Helen: Well, he can't play anyway, can he, Tanim?

Tanim: Why don't we give him another chance?

Helen: No, we don't want an old slowcoach playing with us. Round Robin, Round Robin!

Jamie: *[getting cross]* Don't be so nasty. He's my friend.

Names and Games

Tanim: Oh, go on, let him.

Helen: No, he can't. Silly Robin Redbreast! Silly Robin Redbreast!

Jamie: *[really angry now]* I think you're being really horrible. I'm not going to play with you any more.

Helen: Don't, then!

Tanim: *[pleading]* Oh yes, do!

Helen: It's nearly the end of playtime anyway. Come on, Tanim, let's see if we can be the first in the line.

[Helen and Tanim go off.]

Robin: Thanks, Jamie. You were really nice.

Jamie: Well, I was getting fed up with 'What's the time, Mr Wolf?' anyway. It's a bit of a baby game, and I never even got to be Mr Wolf.

Robin: Will you play with me now, then?

Jamie: It all depends.

Robin: Depends on what?

Jamie: On whether you're going to boss me about all the time.

Robin: I won't, I promise. I know, you can choose which game to play.

Jamie: All right then.

[There is a pause while Jamie thinks.]

Robin: Remember, if there's anyone called Robin in it I have to be him, because my name really is Robin.

Jamie: *[looking pleased]* That's just given me a brilliant idea.

[The bell rings.]

Jamie: Oh, there's the bell.

Robin: Never mind, we can play it tomorrow. What is it?

Jamie: Batman and Robin!

[He runs off, followed more slowly by Robin who is looking thoughtful.]

happy birthday

Birthday Surprise

Ten parts
(Can be expanded to include a whole class)

Suitable for middle primary

Characters

Stuart
(the birthday boy)

Stuart's mum

Mr E

Rachel

Children — When all the children are speaking you will see this symbol

Joe

Ajax

Look out for the symbols to show you who's speaking!

Jaswinder

Ellen

David

Samantha

106

[Stuart is in his sitting room with Mum and some of his friends, including Ajax, Samantha, Ellen and Joe. There is a table with a floor-length cloth on it. Under this a toy rabbit must be hidden.]

Mum: Well, nearly everyone's here. Shall we start the party games?

Stuart: I don't want to play games. I want to have tea.

Mum: We can't have tea till everyone's here. Shall we play The Farmer's in his Den?

Children: Yes!

Stuart: No, that's stupid.

Mum: You can be the farmer, Stuart, as it's your birthday.

Birthday Surprise

Stuart: I don't want to be the farmer.
I want to be the dog.

Mum: All right, then – you be the farmer, Ajax. Off you go.

Children: *[in a circle]* The farmer's in his den. The farmer's in his den. Ee, I, Ee, I, the farmer's in his den.

[The doorbell rings.]

Mum: There's the doorbell. I'll go. You carry on playing.

[Mum goes out.]

Children: The farmer wants a wife. The farmer wants a wife. Ee, I, Ee, I, the farmer wants a wife.

[Mum comes in with Rachel.]

Mum: It's Rachel, Stuart.

Rachel: Happy birthday, Stuart.

Stuart: Where's my present?

Mum: Stuart, don't be so greedy!

Rachel: Here you are, Stuart.

Stuart: *[unwrapping the present]* It's not very big. It's a book. That's boring!

Mum: Stuart, don't be so rude! Thank you very much, Rachel. Would you like to play The Farmer's in his Den?

Rachel: Yes, please.

[Rachel joins the circle.]

Joe: Who are you going to choose for your wife, Ajax?

Ajax: Samantha.

[The doorbell rings again.]

Mum: There's the bell again. I'll go. You carry on playing.

[Mum goes out.]

Children: The wife wants a child. The wife wants a child. Ee, I, Ee, I, the wife wants a child.

[Mum comes in with David.]

Mum: It's David, Stuart.

Stuart: Where's my present?

Mum: Stuart, really!

David: Here you are, Stuart.

Stuart: [unwrapping the present] I know what this is. A boring old football. I've got one already.

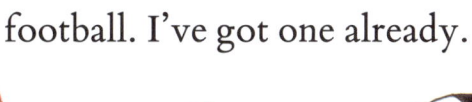

Mum: Stuart, don't be so rude! Thank you very much, David. Would you like to play The Farmer's in his Den?

Stuart: Yes, please.

[David joins the circle.]

Ajax: Who are you going to choose for your child, Samantha?

Samantha: Ellen.

[The doorbell rings again.]

Mum: That must be Jaswinder. She's the last one. I'll go. You carry on playing.

[Mum goes out.]

	Stuart:	It's not fair. I want to be the child. It's my birthday.
	Samantha:	You said you wanted to be the dog.
	Stuart:	I'm sick of this boring game anyway. I want to have tea.

[Mum comes in with Jaswinder.]

	Mum:	It's Jaswinder, Stuart. Now, do be polite.
	Jaswinder:	Happy birthday, Stuart.
	Stuart:	Where's my present?
	Mum:	STUART! BEHAVE YOURSELF!

Birthday Surprise

Jaswinder: Here you are, Stuart.

Stuart: *[opening the present]* It feels like a car. Yes, it is. Is it radio-controlled?

Jaswinder: No.

Stuart: It's boring, then.

Mum: If you go on like this you'll go up to your room and have no birthday cake. Thank you very much, Jaswinder. Everyone's here, then.

[The doorbell rings again.]

Mum: Who can that be? I'll go and see.

[Mum goes out.]

Ellen: What are we having for tea, Stuart?

Stuart: Mum wouldn't let me see. I bet there are cucumber sandwiches. I hate them.

Ajax: What sort of cake have you got?

Stuart: I don't know. I bet it's a boring old round one.

[Mum comes in.]

Mum: Children, I've got a very special surprise for you. Everyone be quiet.

Stuart: I don't want a surprise, I want tea.

Mum: Not yet, Stuart. Now, when you're all quiet the conjuror will come in.

Stuart: I don't want a conjuror, I want—

Children: BE QUIET!

[Mum opens the door and Mr E comes in.]

Mr E: Good afternoon, my friends. My name is Mister E.

Stuart: That's a stupid name.

Rachel: What does the E stand for?

Mr E: Aha, it's a mystery.

Mum: Mystery, Mister E – that's funny, isn't it? Now, children, you sit and watch Mr E's show while I get the tea on the table.

[Mum goes out. The children sit on the floor.]

Mr E: Now, my friends, my magic wand is telling me that one of you has a birthday today.

Stuart: I bet it was my mum who told you, not your wand at all.

Mr E: It's you, isn't it? You're the one.

Stuart: So what?

Mr E: So I am inviting you to help me perform Trick One!

Stuart: I don't want to.

Mr E: Very well, I shall choose again. What is your name, young friend?

Rachel: Rachel.

Mr E: Would you like to help me perform Trick One, Rachel?

Rachel: Yes, please.

Mr E: Then step forward and hold this hat while I wave my wand. Would our other friends like to help me say the magic spell?

Children: Yes!

Stuart: No.

Mr E: [tapping the magic hat] Very well, repeat after me: Abracadabra and rat-tat-tat, What's inside the magic hat?

Children: Abracadabra and rat-tat-tat, What's inside the magic hat?

Mr E: I'm ready to grab it. I think it's a . . .

Birthday Surprise

[He puts his hand into the hat and pulls out a rabbit.]

Children: **RABBIT!** *[They clap.]*

Stuart: That's stupid. Anyone could do that. I bet you couldn't make a *monster* come out of the hat.

Mr E: We shall see, but first I shall need a new helper. What is your name, young friend?

Joe: Joe.

Mr E: Would you like to help me perform Trick Two, Joe?

Joe: Yes, please.

Mr E: Then step forward and take the hat from Rachel, if you please. Are you ready for the next spell, my friends?

Birthday Surprise

Children: Yes!

Stuart: I bet it will be the same as the last one.

Mr E: Abracadabra and vampire bat,
What's inside the magic hat?

Children: Abracadabra and vampire bat,
What's inside the magic hat?

Mr E: It's coming to get us.

[Some of the children back away.]

Mr E: I think it's a . . .

[He puts in his hand and pulls out a lettuce.]

Children: LETTUCE! *[They laugh.]*

Stuart: That's stupid. You said it would be a monster.

Mr E: Aha, I was tricking you! I told you it was a trick, didn't I?

David: The rabbit will like the lettuce, anyway.

Stuart: I bet it was in the hat all the time.

Mr E: Let us move on to Trick Three and a new helper. What is your name, young friend?

Ellen: Ellen.

Mr E: Would you like to help me perform Trick Three, Ellen?

Ellen: Yes, please.

Stuart: It's not fair; I want to be the helper. It's my birthday.

Mr E: Very well, as Trick Three is such a tricky trick, I shall have two helpers instead of one. Step forward, Stuart and Ellen. I need one of you to go under that table.

Stuart: I will! It's my birthday.
[He goes under the table.]

Mr E: Are you ready for the next spell, my young friends?

Children: Yes!

Mr E: Abracadabra and Auntie Mabel, What is under the magic table?

Children: Abracadabra and Auntie Mabel, What is under the magic table?

Mr E: Now, Ellen, I need you to look under the table.

Birthday Surprise

[Ellen goes behind the table and lifts the cloth.]

Mr E: Get ready to grab it. I think it's a . . .

[Ellen pulls a rabbit out from under the table.]

Children: **RABBIT!** *[They clap.]*

Joe: Where's Stuart?

Ellen: He's not there any more.

David: He must have turned into the rabbit!

[Enter Mum.]

Mum:		Are you enjoying the show, children?
Children:		Yes!
Mum:		The birthday tea's ready. *[She looks around.]* Where's Stuart?
Ellen:		*[holding the rabbit]* Here he is.
Mum:		Don't be silly – that's a rabbit.
Ajax:		Yes – Stuart's turned into a rabbit.
Mum:		Do stop joking. Where is he?
Mr E:		He is here in front of your eyes, madam. So very nice and quiet.

Birthday Surprise

Mum: Oh no! This is terrible! I want my little boy back.

Mr E: Do not fear, madam. He will change back in an hour or so.

Mum: Are you sure?

Mr E: As sure as my name is Mr E.

Mum: And are you sure he'll be exactly the same as before?

Mr E: More or less, madam, more or less.

Mum: *[alarmed]* **What do you mean, more or less?**

Mr E: I just mean he might be a little bit . . . different.

Mum: Different? In what way?

Mr E: Well, usually with Trick Three the children end up just a little bit . . . nicer.

Children: Hooray!

Samantha: But do we have to wait an hour for our tea?

Mum: No, let's have it now. It should be nice and peaceful. Would you like to have some tea too, Mr E?

Mr E: Yes, please, madam. And perhaps our rabbit friends would like to come too.

Jaswinder: Do rabbits like birthday cake?

Mr E: No, my friend, but there is one thing which they love.

David: What's that?

Mr E: Cucumber sandwiches!

[They all go out of the room to have tea.]

Putting on a Play

Tips for actors:

- Practice makes perfect, so rehearse before your big performance. It's fun to do some warm-up exercises and games before the rehearsal, to prepare your body and mind for your acting roles.

- Practise your lines and ask someone to test you as you learn them.

- Knowing who speaks before you and listening to what they say is called a cue. It's important to know when you should speak, so remember to learn your cues too.

- Think about how your character is feeling. That will help you say the lines with the right expression.

- It's also a good idea to think about how your character moves. Perhaps you are acting someone older or younger than yourself, or even an animal, so try out some different ways of walking and gesturing till you find something that feels right.

- Even professional actors sometimes forget their lines, so make sure that there is a "prompt" just offstage, near enough for the actors to hear but out of sight of the audience.

- Maybe your family or friends have come to see the show, but try to resist the temptation to look for them in the audience or wave to them!

- Don't forget to take a big bow at the end. This is called a "curtain call", and needs a little practice as well, so that it doesn't look ragged.

Activities

Posters

Make sure people know your play is happening so you get a nice big audience! A good way to do this is to create some posters that say where the play is being staged and when it will start.

Tickets

Why not design tickets for your audience? Someone can be in charge of checking tickets when people arrive.

Programmes

You might like to make programmes for your audience. Fold a piece of paper in half and then write the name of the play and the playwright on the front and decorate it. That's the cover. Inside, write a list of the scenes and another one of the characters and who is

About the Author

Julia Donaldson is the author of some of the world's best-loved children's books, including modern classics *The Gruffalo* and *The Gruffalo's Child*, *The Snail and the Whale* and the What the Ladybird Heard adventures. Julia also writes fiction, including the Princess Mirror-Belle books illustrated by Lydia Monks, as well as poems, plays and songs – and her brilliant live shows are always in demand. She was Children's Laureate 2011–13 and has been honoured with a CBE for Services to Literature. Julia lives in Sussex with two tabby cats.

About the Illustrator

Kate Pankhurst lives in Leeds with her family and spotty dog, Olive. She has a studio based in an old spinning mill where she writes and illustrates children's books. Her projects have included the Fantastically Great Women series and Mariella Mystery Investigates series. Kate is distantly related to the suffragette Emmeline Pankhurst, something that has been an influence on the type of books she enjoys creating for children.

playing them. You should also add the names of people who have helped in other ways, like the director, if you have one, or perhaps the costume designer.

Snacks

Why not make some treats for the cast, or some for the audience, who could eat them in the interval (if you have one) or after the show.

A Sequel?

If you've enjoyed taking part in your play, perhaps you'd like to have a go at being a playwright yourself. You could try writing a sequel, maybe with the same characters or introducing some new ones. Writing a play can be more fun than writing a story, as you don't need to bother with all the descriptive bits, just on what the characters are saying, which is called the dialogue, and what they are doing, which is called the stage directions.